AF399662

Stella Canis and Other Short Stories

Stella Canis

and

Other Short Stories

Predrag Mihajlović

© Predrag Mihajlović 2019
Förlag: BoD Books on Demand, Stockholm, Sverige
Tryck: BoD Books on Demand, Norderstedt, Tyskland
ISBN: 9789176993149

Stella Canis

and

Other Short Stories

English Translation by
Avison Communication AB
www.avison.se

Stella Canis and Other Short Stories

If we hadn't forgotten to lock the door, I'm certain that none of it would have happened.

(from *The Apatride and the Confused Dog*)

Stella Canis and Other Short Stories

Contents

Stella Canis and Other Short Stories

No One is Responsible

"Good day, Mrs. Grankvist!"

The police inspector expressed his welcome in a quiet, compassionate voice. He carefully extended his hand toward the woman, who was wearing a long, black winter coat.

"Good afternoon."

The woman's response was so quiet that the inspector found it easier to read the greeting on her pale lips than by listening to her voice.

"Please sit down."

He motioned for her to sit down before they stopped shaking hands.

"Thank you."

They let each other's hands go as she thanked him.

"My name is Tristram Lind."

"Tristram?"

The woman spoke just as quietly as when she said hello. She looked down at the table. Inspector Lind had a hard time telling if the woman was just routinely repeating his first name or if it was a reaction to its rarity. In the end he decided it was the latter.

"Yes, really."

His response was almost apologetic, and he wondered if it would be appropriate to explain how he had gotten his unusual name.

"An unusual name."

"It is, yes."

His voice grew a bit livelier when he confirmed the woman's comment. He considered whether it would make for a less painful conversation if he opened it by giving a brief background of his name. The woman was still looking down at the desk as the inspector spoke.

"There are unusual things going on, too."

This time his emphasis was on the phrase *unusual things*. At the same time, he attempted a guarded smile. He purposely waited a moment before speaking another sentence, so that the phrase he emphasized would settle in the woman's consciousness.

"I got it from my grandmother. It's from the name of the protagonist in an old English novel called *Tristram Shandy* by Laurence Sterne."

"Tristram, it's got a nice ring to it. How nice that your grandmother chose it and that your parents accepted her suggestion."

"Yes, I'm very grateful to my grandmother and to my parents for that."

"It's always good not to lose sight of our most tender feelings and the feeling of close-ness to our children and parents. And our grandparents too, if they're still alive."

The room grew quiet for a while.

It was nearly two minutes before the woman broke the silence.

"Today is the November 26th."

Only then did she lift her head and look at the inspector.

"Yes, the year is 195- I might add."

"And now a week has gone by."

"Exactly, ma'am."

He moved the hands he was resting on his knees to the edge of the table after confirming what she had said.

The woman followed his movement as if she expected him to start looking for something in the notepad on the table to his left.

He didn't do that.

"I presume you have come to some conclusion."

"Yes, we have."

Mrs. Grankvist exhaled faintly after hearing the answer she had wanted to hear.

"So how did my daughter die? Was she murdered?"

"She was killed, ma'am."

"Killed?"

"Yes, you might put it that way."

"Put it that way?"

The inspector could sense mild irritation in her voice, even though she had spoken these four words very slowly. She was a single mother whose only daughter was now dead, and he knew not to blurt out the answer too fast. Not having to get to the answer in a hurry suited him just fine – he was a man who had a hard time getting straight to the point. He was aware of this trait. Because of it, over the years he had developed a strategy that caused his interlocutors to do so themselves – to tell or express the thing it was his job to tell or express.

"Mrs. Grankvist, I understand that what I am going to tell you will sound unreal, to say the least."

"My reality has already become unreal, nor do I have any real hope now. The only thing you need to do now is to speak in your officialese to tell me how my daughter died and who is responsible for her death."

"I understand."

"I <u>have</u> to know how my daughter died and who is responsible for her death. That is all I need in life."

Another brief silence fell, and this time it was Tristram's turn to look down at the table.

"That's the odd thing. There is no one who is responsible for your daughter's…"

"No one is responsible? But you said she was killed?"

"Yes, she was…"

"And you know who did it, right?"

"We do. We know what took her life…"

"*What,* not *who*?

"That's what the experts say."

"The experts? And what do you say?"

"I have no reason to contradict them."

"Does that mean that my daughter's boyfriend has been freed from all suspicion?"

"The suspicions against him were fairly weak from the start."

"Isn't it true that they met for the last time on November 18, or rather that night, and that she was found very early in the morning, life-less, lying in a field at the edge of the city right by the country road where she had parked her car?"

"Quite right…"

Mrs. Grankvist's voice began to tremble more and more as she continued speaking.

"She had a head injury, a wound caused by a heavy blow with a blunt object, probably a rock, right?"

"That's right ma'am…"

"So who hit her? She can't very well have done it herself."

"No, Mrs. Grankvist. Pulling off something like that is quite unlikely."

"So is there anything even more unlikely?"

"I'm afraid there is..."

"What? A meteorite, perhaps?!"

"Exactly!"

No one cares

"Did you know that all the talk about the motion of the stars and the planets and their influence on our lives is just as meaningless and ineffectual as all the discussions of the existence and nonexistence of time? That it is we humans who not only create, but also manipulate all of these concepts and the relationships between them and their various influences on us? That we are very good constructors, my friend?"

That was the philosophical introduction to an amusing story that a friend of mine started telling me a few years ago. We were at a restaurant one very cold and snowy winter and were on our fourth or fifth beer when he spoke those words.

"I did not know that," I answered, leaning comfortably against a radiator right behind me.

"I knew you didn't. Then my next question is: Do you know why? I know your answer because you could not answer my first question."

"Why?" I asked, scarcely interested, since I figured my friend was already under the influence of the more than two liters of beer he had downed.

"It's just to meet or satisfy their needs!" he answered in a slightly louder voice. "To achieve their goals no matter what kind of goal they want to achieve."

"What's so bad about that?" I wondered in the same loud voice.

"Nothing", he replied, tapping the table gently with his knuckles. "It's not always a bad thing. I just want to say that it's a matter of manipulation. For example, I came into the world and I exist in it thanks to a manipulation."

"You were born through a manipulation?" I asked a bit cheekily.

"Not exactly, but I have a patriarch or some other high-ranking church official to thank for the fact that I exist today."

"How is that, my friend?"

"Do you really want to know?"

"Is there anything more important right now?"

"Okay, I'll tell you. The year would have been 1930. My grandmother was nearly 23 years old when her father decided to marry her off to my future grandfather. A few years before that, my grandmother had been in love (as she told me) with someone that she had had to keep secret from her father. She and the young man used to meet surreptitiously in a plum orchard. They probably kissed there and sometimes they drank plum brandy – Slivovitz, it's usually called (my grandmother told me that). At some point the relationship ended and I never found out how.

So when my grandmother was almost 23 – back then you were considered old if you were unmarried at that age – her father and the father of my future grandfather decided that the two of them should marry. I don't know if my grandfather was reluctant about the match, but my grandmother was probably reluctant to marry him, but no one cared much about that. But there was a little issue, an obstacle standing in the way of their arranged marriage. The fact, that is, that my grandmother was six years older than her future husband, a tall and handsome youth, which meant that he was not yet of age and that such a marriage would not be permitted by law."

"Now things are starting to get interesting," I said and made a sign to the waiter to bring us two more beers.

"You're right about that. The next installment of this story will hardly be dull. It would be almost another year before my grandfather reached the age of maturity and their fathers did not want to wait that long. I have no idea why they were in such a hurry. What I learned for certain is that my grandmother was not pregnant. Neither by her ex-boyfriend nor her future husband. Like I said, I have no idea what sort of problem my grandfather was facing that meant that they could not wait a year to get married. In any case, there was a problem to solve. And it didn't take very long to come up with a brilliant idea. The two fathers then composed a letter to the patriarch.

They awaited his reply intently. It was no more than three weeks before the patriarch's reply arrived by mail. The problem was solved and the marriage was sanctioned. Eventually they had children, including the boy who was to be my father, who in turn married my future mother, and eventually I came into the world."

My friend broke off his story abruptly.

"So what did the letter say?" I asked my friend, who was looking groggily at the table and appeared not to notice that he had left a gap in his story.

"The patriarch's?"

"No," I said with a laugh. "I understand that the patriarch's reply was positive for the two fathers. What did it say in the letter that your forefathers wrote to that patriarch?"

"They simply asked him to let my grandmother lend 11 months of her life to my grandfather so that he could reach the age of majority and marry her," my friend answered as he raised his mug in a toast.

I looked at him with sympathy for a moment and then said:

"You're right, who cares about the motion of the planets."

I raised my glass and took a long swig of beer.
He did the same.

Stella Canis (Dog Day Afternoon)

There was a devoted and conscientious middle-aged family man who had a summer cottage on the outskirts of the city.

It was a Sunday in late July, just when the mercury had reached its daytime high – just when the small garden plots were bursting with many different kinds of ripe vegetables. The man had just such a garden plot at his summer cottage. Because he and his wife had now reached the age where people start to think more and more seriously about their health, it was entirely expected that most of their conversations that day revolved around a vegetarian theme. The man's wife hit upon an idea for what to cook for an early dinner.

"A pumpkin pie!" she said.

But she needed a pumpkin, and their little plot had plenty of fine pumpkins.

"Sure thing! I'll drive out and fetch a nice pumpkin," said the man.

Not only because he was a husband who was always pleased to cater to his wife's wishes, but because he had a craving for a tasty pumpkin pie. And his wife could whip one up! So the man did not find it difficult to get up from the summer chair in which he was comfortably seated and to give up the cool shade of the porch for the rays of the blazing sun.

The whole chore wouldn't take more than 15 minutes, and if he drove a little faster he could even be back home in ten minutes. He got in the car, started the engine and drove out to his summer cottage.

No sooner said than done! Scarcely five minutes later he pulled off the road. He was soaked in sweat when he got out of the car, since the AC was out of order. He took off his short-sleeved shirt and used it to wipe the sweat off his face and chest before tossing it in the car and walking toward the fence. It always took a long time to unlock the gate in the wooden fence, so he decided to jump it. As he did so, he saw a broken beer bottle in the gully that ran along the fence. The rays of the sun reflected in the sharp brick-colored shards. He thought to pick them up, but he changed his mind and walked off with the intention of returning to pick them up later. He jumped the fence and entered the yard.

He needed a pretty big pumpkin. Suddenly he sensed a smell that only he knew. It was a smell he knew from childhood. The smell of a snake, as he called it, although he was unsure if you could actually smell a snake. It could be likened to the smell of an unripe peach. Every time he had smelled that smell he had had a stroke of bad luck. He experienced a deep and short-lived sense of unease and started turning about, left and right, in an attempt to see if there was anything nearby that might cause any un-pleasantness. But he could not discern anything of the kind. All about him there was only heat and silence.

"A real dog day!" he said aloud to himself, then wiped the sweat from his brow with his palm, bent down, picked a suitable pumpkin and walked quickly back to his car.

At which point things started going all wrong. The man was holding the pumpkin in his left hand while using his right to steady himself against the fence as he tried to jump it. Mid-jump, his right hand inexplicably gave way, and he went reeling into the gully on the other side of the fence. A sharp pain in his right foot forced him upright immediately. The blood was almost the color of pitch. It covered his whole foot and he could not see how big the wound was. Carefully, so as to avoid hurting his left leg, he used his good leg to hop to the car, grabbed his shirt, and used it to quickly wrap his injured foot. The most important thing, he thought, was to get home as quickly as possible, disinfect the wound and dress it.

He started the car and began to drive. He held the steering wheel with one hand and the pumpkin with the other.

The next instant, he lost hold of the pumpkin. It rolled down under his legs. Instinctively, he bent down and tried to fetch it back up. At which point he lost control of the steering wheel, sending the car down into a ditch. Now the unfortunate man experienced a strong pain in his right hand. He realized right away that it was broken.

Cradling the pumpkin in his left hand, he tried to use his good leg to open the passenger side door, since the door on his side was pressed up against the ditch and would not open. He succeeded. Like a lizard, he crawled out of the car with the pumpkin in his hand. And then he made a new mistake. Forgetting that his right foot was injured, he tried to rest his weight on it. A shock of pain threw him backwards and he hit his head on the part of the car where the edges of the door meet. At which point he passed out.

As these things usually go, he only regained consciousness at the hospital. He felt no pain. He just felt a little bit cold, but otherwise comfortable. Like most people, he was also very familiar with the smell of hospitals, and he did not need to open his eyes to understand where he was. He just lay there in bed for a while, cursing himself silently.

When he opened his eyes, he recognized his dear wife's face. She was looking at him silently, anxiously. And he looked at her. It felt as if their gaze had been going on forever. Suddenly the woman's face clouded. She stared toward the man's belly. He wondered what could have prompted the change in her.

Maybe it's not my wife, he thought. And if it is my wife, then maybe I am someone else. And vice versa – that is how his thinking went.

"Why are you laughing?" asked his wife, ending his dilemma.

"I don't know," the man replied.

"What happened? Do you feel up to telling me?" asked the woman as a few tears streamed down her face.

He felt up to it.

When he had finished telling the story of what happened, he noticed his wife looking in the direction of his belly again. The man could clearly see the fury in his wife's eyes. When she unexpectedly reached out for his stomach, he was frightened that she was going to punch him there. Them he saw the pumpkin in her hands. He had been cradling it against his stomach with his left arm the whole time.

The woman looked around the room and then disappeared. When she returned she was holding not only the pumpkin but also a knife. She calmly got down on her knees. He could see the hand holding the knife bobbing up and down energetically. The pumpkin was cut into many pieces.

"There!" said the woman calmly, then patted her hair into place, put the knife back where she had found it, walked back into the room and sat down happily by her husband's bed.

32

The Indefinite Position of the Full Moon

I am a very chatty, open and sociable person. If I'm sitting on a bus, a train, a plane or in a waiting room at a hospital or some other public setting, I have a hard time just sitting there all sleepy and silent. I have a look around and try to catch the attention of one of the passengers or the people waiting and try to start a conversation. I have always been like that and there is nothing I can do about it.

I am aware that it can be annoying to some people and I have tried to be more reserved, but it's tough. If the moon is full, I've noticed, it's impossible to contain myself. It's not like I remember afterwards what I talked to people about. The act of conversing itself leaves me satisfied, and the substance of what is said and heard disappears as soon as I disappear or my interlocutor does. At least that's the way it was up to three months ago.

It was a day, or rather a night, in December last year. After a short vacation (five days) in Greece, I was on my way back to Stockholm. It was already evening when the plane took off. I was sitting by the aisle, and sitting next to me was an older gentleman looking out the window. The seats in front of us were occupied by a woman and her daughter, who I would put at 18 years old. To their right sat her husband with the other child, a boy who I guessed was 13 or 14. Behind us sat two odd characters who immediately started reading when they took their seats. Across the aisle to my right there was no one, all the seats were empty. So my best chances of starting to communicate with someone was to talk to my immediate neighbor. The problem was that he was looking through the window as raptly as if he were expecting to see an unidentified flying object.

Only after about half an hour did he turn to face me unexpectedly and say:

"Look at the full moon!"

I hunched to see it and I made my move conspicuous to show that I was prepared for a conversation.

"How festive!" I said.

For a moment I was a bit worried if I had chosen my words wisely. *Festive* could sound a bit over the top, and the man might get the impression that I was being ironic.

"Stupendous! Quixotic!" the man said with delight.

When he used these words, words that were somewhat unusual to me, especially *quixotic,* the floodgates opened in me.

"I don't remember ever seeing such a beautiful, impressive and crystal clear moon!" I exclaimed, almost yelling.

"Exactly!"

After confirming what I had said, he took off his eyeglasses and wiped them off. When he put them back on he added another observation.

"It almost feels as if you can't tell whether it is up above us or below us, whether it is up or down."

That was not at all my impression and I wondered how he could come up with such an absurd statement. Certainly I didn't want to oppose him, since that would lead our conversation down the wrong path. Nor could I say that what he said was true and that I shared his impression. I thought feverishly about what to say without taking too much time – I didn't want to risk the chat we had started coming to an abrupt end.

"It's not up there but down there, it's not down there but up there." I pronounced the words in an almost singsong voice and without quite thinking them through.

"What is that supposed to mean?" he asked.

I could not sense any mocking or emotional coldness in the tone of his voice, only a keen interest.

"What you said brought back an association from my early childhood. Very early childhood."

"Tell me," he said.

He seemed genuinely interested in hearing my short tale.

"It was a very long time ago."

I paused briefly and nodded thoughtfully.

"It was in the early sixties," I went on, "and I was a shade less than three years old. My parents and I lived in a small town where there was only one paved street. There was a little girl living in our neighborhood. She was around my age. I still remember that her name was Adriana, even though it was over 50 years ago. We played together often, but of course I can't remember the games we played. Except for one thing! For some reason we used to walk up and down the street hugging one another. And we sang! As we walked down the street we sang:

'It's not down but up.' And as we walked up the street we sang 'It's not up but down!' I remember her smile very clearly. It was a sympathetic smile in spite of her teeth being full of cavities. I remember it...as if it were yesterday."

"How long were you friends?"

"It was just that summer. She and her family moved somewhere else that same August, I would guess."

"Did you ever see each other afterwards?"

"No, truth be told."

"It's odd that you didn't try to find her when you were older, since you seem never to have forgotten that little girl."

"Just a few years after they had moved, I heard from my mother that she had died. An acquaintance had told her."

"The little girl? What a shame! How sad! What happened? Did you ever learn why she died?"

"According to what my mother had heard, she drowned in a river. The river was called the Drina and it was notorious back then."

The man was silent and was again looking at the full moon shining bright.

I was doing the same thing.

We sat mostly in silence for the rest of the flight.

When we landed at the airport it was time to bid my neighbor adieu. Before getting up from my seat I let the woman and her family get up and start heading for the exit. First her husband walked by, then the children and finally the woman. I felt vaguely annoyed because it was taking the woman a long time to walk past me. I usually disembarked the plane very quickly after a trip had ended.

Once she had finally made it by, I got up and took my little suitcase down from the overhead bin. When I turned around, I saw a piece of paper on the floor. I bent down quickly to pick it up. I gave it a quick glance. My friendly fellow passenger wondered what it was for. I told him that it was just a bit of paper and nothing more, crumpling it in my hand to give the impression that I was going to throw it away.

Once I had made it off the plane and was on my way to the train I looked at the note again.

This is what it said:

"That little girl is alive."

Under the Starry Sky

Eternity should be understood as a relative term when I say that it was a clear summer evening an eternity ago.

I was lying in a dark green meadow and looking deeply into the starlit sky. Suddenly I got the impression that I was deep inside it, in a weightless state. It wasn't just that – I noticed that wherever I turned my head and wherever I directed my gaze, I could see different fragments of time from my life. I could switch from one time to another from my past, but also from the time I saw myself in to another. All of these life fragments were enticing and nice to see, but the most enticing time of all seemed to be early childhood.

So I turned my head to my left and looked back 100 years in time and clearly saw the following:

I'm two years old. It's an early autumn morning. Sunday. We - my father and I - are out in the country visiting his parents, and are just about to leave their house. As we walk past a tall old oak, a cute little black pig runs towards us. My father quickly picks it up and carefully tosses it into a puddle to his left. As the little pig easily swims out of the puddle, the two of us laugh, father and son. I am standing on my father's right and craning my neck to look at him: tall, with an athlete's build, dark-haired, wearing a white shirt and a dark suit. I laugh out loud and feel a tremendous sense of pride and joy at being with my dad. Dad keeps on laughing for as long as I look at him. My gaze fixes on his pearly-white teeth. This causes me to turn my gaze toward my grandparents' little house, toward what I had experienced less than half an hour earlier: I'm sitting on my grandfather's knee as he is sitting on the stone doorstep, playing tambourine and smiling lovingly at me. His smile is adorned by a short, well-groomed mustache and pearly-white teeth.

I quickly turn my gaze to the right and look 21 years into the future from the pig in the puddle and see and hear myself telling my father about this memory.

"And you remember that, my boy?"

"Yes, Dad, I sure do."

There is no doubt that he is impressed by my memory. He frowns and says with a nod:

"Yes, your grandfather had all his teeth when he died, aged 52, a few months after that. That was the last time you saw him. "

"Yeah, I have a good memory," I say to him.

Then I turn my gaze just over 21 years back in time from the conversation I had with my dad:

I am just over two years old and am standing outside our narrow and dilapidated two-story house. It is a silent, hot summer morning. The overcast sky makes the air feel suffocating.

Suddenly I feel as if I am about to lose my balance. I don't understand what is happening but I get very scared.

I start screaming:

"Mommy! Mommy!"

My mom rushes out of the house and calls for me. I don't understand anything she says or is trying to tell me, but I well understand the fear in her slanted Japanese eyes and see the spasm in her beautiful face. I run to her.

The next moment we are standing on the house's wooden doorstep, and I feel calm and safe in my mom's protecting embrace. While leaning against her knees, I see a bit of brick come tumbling down from the ceiling and hit the exact spot where I had been standing a few seconds earlier.

I quickly turn my gaze 23 years into the future from the earthquake I had been through. I tell my mom about what happened, about the earthquake we had been through together.

"And you remember it?" my mom asks, doubtless impressed by my memory.

"Yes, Mom, I sure do."

She then immediately adds:

"My nickname back then was actually 'the Japanese one', since I had slanted eyes."

"I remember my life's first earthquake. It was with you, Mom. "

Mom smiles at me.

I smile back and say:

"I remember everything that happened for the first time in my life."

Suddenly floating up there in the sky, I turned my gaze down earthward and looked down at my tombstone. I could see it so clearly under the billions of twinkling stars. They shone on the peaceful and serene time in the Balkans. It was a beautiful sight.

The Only World

The yellow moonbeams were transformed into silvery tones when they fell on the drops of seawater that slowly ran down Noriko Shimada's naked body that night.

The water came up to her knees when I spotted her, and I could not take my eyes off the dreamlike body that suddenly appeared before me. I stood there as if enchanted, no more than fifteen yards away. I thought she had already bathed, since her body was wet and because she was now looking at the moon and enjoying the magical sight. No stars could be seen, only the moon, big as the sun, in the endless sky above the endless sea. The sky, the moon, the sun and Noriko Shimada's naked body! The picture I was expecting to see absolutely couldn't fit with the one I had in front of me.

I could neither see her face nor any possible kindness in it, nor her eyes and any possible intellectual depth in them, but the moonbeams that poured through her body and then hit me made it possible to scan all of this and feel nothing but admiration for the woman. I didn't know her name, that is something I would learn later.

Just 15 minutes before I had been sitting at a pub drinking my third mojito. For the sake of learning the language, I was eavesdropping on people speaking Japanese to the right and left of me at the bar. It turned out that my Japanese was at a much lower level than I had thought. Reading short texts while listening to them on CDs at the same time proved to be a misguided approach. At least for me. But you have to start somewhere. The music was just loud enough and I could clearly hear a couple standing to my right talking about the lunar eclipse. Despite the music not interfering with my eavesdropping attempt, I misunderstood and thought that the lunar eclipse was going to happen soon.

"Hai!" I said in Japanese in a loud and happy voice, gently striking the bar with my fist. I was thinking of a highly suitable location to witness the eclipse. I drained my mojito, settled the bill with my debit card, and headed out into the night with hands atremble, already under the influence of what I had had to drink. It took me scarcely 15 minutes of brisk walking to get to the little beach I had seen on a long afternoon walk I had gone on that same day.

Now I was standing there delightedly looking at the mysterious woman's enchantingly naked, wet body, her back turned toward me. She stooped down a bit towards the water and used both hands to cup seawater and lave it over herself, on her arms and the breasts I had an irresistible urge to see. I wanted to be the water flowing over her skin. I stood there, motionless and mute, as if paralyzed by ecstasy.

The first brief scene unfolding in front of me solidified in my brain: it was as if I was no longer able to follow the slow sequence of events. My imagination was set into instant, vigorous motion, as never before with a woman as its object. I, who had never been married and had never had any conscious thought of starting a family, of wife and children, now very clearly saw this woman as my wedded wife. I saw our three children, saw them laughing as we happily looked down at their pretty, small and shiny teeth and their beautifully-formed eyes, black and slightly slanted. What I saw felt so real, so compelling. My impression was that my life could only be this way and that there could be no alternative. There was a world that I was in, and no parallel worlds could be considered except for the one under that moon. Nor were there any stars that I could dream my way to. We stood resolutely on Earth, illuminated by its lovely satellite.

Then I noticed something odd. My eyebrows furrowed. It seemed as if the delightful image that had been seared into my brain was beginning to distance itself from me. Slowly but surely, the distance between Noriko and me grew greater and greater. That goddess-like body, that superior body, was no longer anywhere to be seen. My eyebrows furrowed even more. Now I could only see her head from the seashore. It too was growing harder and harder to see. I approached closer to the water, but my confusion did not diminish. The next moment, as things grew darker and darker around me, a gust of wind hit me like a slap in the face. I gave a start and only then did I understand what was happening. I finally jumped into the water and started swimming furiously for the woman, whose head had already slipped beneath the surface of the water.

"If you hadn't made it out in time to save me, if you hadn't managed to thwart my suicide attempt, I would never have had these three happy children. Or you", my wife Noriko likes to say every now and then before she gives me a loving kiss.

"That night I swam not only for your life, I also did it for my life, for our life and for our children's lives", is what I usually say at those times, as I lovingly kiss her back.

Vittorio Vespucci's Smile

"Vittorio, there is something I'm wondering about, or rather have been wondering about for several years now, every time you enter my thoughts. And enter them you have, believe me. I wonder why you never reacted negatively when we called you an alien. You never showed signs of getting sad or annoyed or angry. That wasn't even the cause of my curiosity. The real cause is that I was surprised at the discreetly ironic, almost mysterious, smile on your face. It's been...how many years have passed since then? Twenty three? Yes, the last time I saw you was in the year 2380, but I have such a clear image of your enigmatic little smile in front of me that it seems like it was yesterday, or at least a week ago. It's like it was imprinted in my memory."

That was the first question I asked my old schoolmate Vittorio Vespucci when we met by chance at a restaurant in Rome, where I had arrived for the first time after working for 10 years at a publishing house in Buenos Aires.

It was I who first recognized him, and who, after quite some hesitation, went up and said hello. The reason for my hesitation is that I did not know how he would react.

There was a group of us high school students back then - Marcelo, Cesare, Ornella (Cesare's girlfriend at the time) - and we literally bullied Vittorio by loudly calling him the Alien. For us it was like his middle name. Vittorio "The Alien" Vespucci. At school he was known as the best student in astronomy, physics and mathematics, but for us he was nothing more than a nerdy and very weird guy who we thought needed constant reminding of the fact. We never used the word ET, since it wouldn't have had the same negative effect. Back then many of us young people liked to watch an ancient film called just that, ET, which would elicit empathy in people if we called him by that name. But we didn't want to offer him any empathy. Oddly enough, he was not hurt by the shameless way we treated him. He never avoided us. On the contrary; he was always around, and he looked at our unruly little gang with great interest, almost admiration. Which always left me a bit bewildered, as it certainly did Marcelo, Cesare and Ornella too, although they never explicitly said so. So now that we had met again and were sitting at the same table as two adults, as serious people, I naturally wanted to apologize to him for the stupid antics that I and my friends had pulled back then.

At the same time, it felt a bit unusual to say sorry to someone who didn't look like he needed it. I wanted to know if his reaction was just a mask, a psychological defense mechanism, or if it was for real. If it was just a mask, I would sincerely beg his forgiveness. If it was for real, I really wanted to know why it was for real. I didn't know if my reasoning was correct, but it seemed perfectly reasonable to me.

I sat and looked at him with remorseful expectation as we waited for our order. Vittorio's face wore the same smile I remember it wearing just over two decades ago.

Then Vittorio started talking.

"That was a good observation, Roberto", he began, nodding slowly. "But it wasn't just irony you were able to read in my face then. I felt sorry for you guys, I even looked down on you a little because of how naïve you were."

"Did you think we were naïve because we called you an alien?" I had to interrupt him and ask this question.

"Exactly, Roberto. It was laughable that you guys called me an alien. It was like an Eskimo calling someone else an Eskimo. Yes, Roberto, all of us were and are aliens", Vittorio said, laughing soundlessly and showing all his teeth.

"Are we all aliens?" I asked, thinking it merely Vittorio's attempt to trivialize the memory of a fatuity from the past.

"Roberto, when we talk about aliens or ETs, how do we imagine them?"

"Either as colonizers or as developers. It's usually the former", I quickly replied to Vittorio's question, adding that I often saw aliens in the negative context, as if they were predators.

"Have you ever thought that we may simply be unconsciously projecting our own characteristics onto beings we have never seen?"

"Actually no, but I understand very well what you are trying to say. I would like to point out that we are now talking about a matter of psychology and philosophy. What I want to say is that I want to know if you have something more concrete to say about this, something more convincing."

"Of course I do, Roberto, and I would like to remind you that I am at least as serious a man as you. So I want you to believe my words when you hear what I want to tell you."

"Vito, believe me when I say that I will believe every word you say here and now."

"All right, Roberto. You know I was an extraordinary pupil at the time. And that extraordinary means extra-extraordinary! As such, I was invited to work for a global scientific organization. A man called Mr. Crocker contacted me. He has now been dead for three years and I can use his real name even if it sounds made-up. He died at the age of one hundred eleven, fifteen years after retiring. I accepted his invitation without any misgivings whatsoever. Now of course it was highly secret, and I was to pretend to attend school and be a regular high school student while I worked for them. I made it through the introductory period just fine, I was highly motivated and my intelligence was equally high.

Back then, they had already discovered and invaded two inhabited planets. The whole process had been going on for 70 years, long enough to move a lot of our people there in secret. Soldiers and scientists. So it wasn't anything new, and I became an active part of this process. The natives there were of course at a much lower level of development than we were, and we were able to easily conquer them when they realized what we were up to. I went there a few times and even learned some of the languages spoken on one of the planets. The language skills I learned were basic, but good enough to be able to understand that they called us aliens. So I don't have to explain that they looked at us the same way as you and many others do when you think of aliens."

At this point Vittorio paused briefly. The robot waiter came with the food and started serving it.

"The process goes on", Roberto said once the robot had left after wishing us a pleasant meal. "I am now a respected man in the organization, and we have managed to destroy yet another planetary life form in order to maintain our own prosperity. I'm not proud of it, but there's no turning back now. I am paying the price for my youthful folly. The ironic smile you guys saw back then is still there today, it's just directed at me now. Roberto, I don't have to say that you mustn't tell anyone. Not because you are not allowed to, but because no one would believe you. And if you do so and they do believe you, I'll deny it. If it's any comfort, you know much more about our kind now."

I just nodded. Silently.

"If you ever meet Marcelo, Cesare and Ornella, tell them hello from me and say that I don't have any unpleasant memories from the time we were just ordinary high school students."

The Little Purple Planet

My last days on earth began the day I saw The Mirror for the first time.

Before that, there had been nothing esoteric in my life. When I looked out before me I didn't see much worth seeing. It could be a table or a TV set or a bare wall if I was sitting at home in the living room. Back then the table was just a table, nothing more. It couldn't, for example, disappear if I wanted it to, it just stood there whether I needed it or not, for example to eat or to write on. Or it could be a tree, a house or empty air if I was out traipsing down the street. Back then the tree was just a tree, nothing more. It couldn't, for example, transform into something else, it just stood there whether or not I needed a spot of shade in which to shelter from the sun for a while.

Then one day I turned around and looked out in front of me again, but in the opposite direction. Then I saw a Mirror.

The Mirror began appearing more and more often. It didn't matter if I was sitting at home in the living room or was out walking in the street.

It was no ordinary Mirror. It reflected neither my figure nor what was behind me, such as a table or a tree. What I saw in that remarkable Mirror was a planet. In terms of form, it looked like any old planet you might see on TV or in a textbook or an atlas. Only its color was different. It was neither blue nor green nor red. It was purple. Now this color did change into different hues depending on what a viewer – that is to say what I – observed. If I looked at the watery surface, it would have a lighter shade. If I looked at the mountainous areas, it took on a darker tone. If I looked at the plains the color would have the shade that is usually associated with the color purple.

But that wasn't the only thing The Mirror offered me. I could see myself living on this little purple planet. There were no people there, but I was not alone either. Living creatures that actually populated this heavenly body were moving around me. They were also purple, but in different shades. Their appearance would change based on my conscious or unconscious desires. They assumed the shapes I wanted. The same went for their behavior. The only thing I could not change about them was their purple color. My entire body also turned purple when I was there, and I wasn't able to do anything about that either.

If I wanted to be alone they would disappear without complaint. They always had something fun to do. I could see myself there alone, see myself swimming in the light purple water, climbing the dark purple mountains, or running on the plains whose color was a conventional shade of purple. Then I felt the same thing outside The Mirror as I felt inside it.

At first I was very suspicious and both standoffish and annoyed at the Mirror, which was starting to appear before me against my own will. With time, once I had realized all the benefits, I just waited for it to appear again. I began staying longer and longer on this planet every time The Mirror appeared. I started feeling at home there, and the planet's people started looking on me more and more as one of their own.

They called me Yn-Tel-Oiv.

"Yn-Tel-Oiv! Yn-Tel-Oiv! Saco-Di-Sra?" they used to shout at me.

(That does not mean "Alien" and it does not mean "How are you doing?")

Pri-Vlig! Pri-Vlig! Gle-Dost! Gle-Dost! I used to respond to them.

(That does not mean "Very well, thank you! How are you doing?")

The other extraordinary thing on that planet was that it was seemingly empty. No houses, streets, roads, no objects… There was so much open space for different creative actions or thoughts. But if I wanted to lie down a bed would appear, if I wanted to sit there would certainly be a chair, if I took a step in any direction a street would appear in front of me, if I wanted a sun and some shade a sun and a tree would appear, if I wanted a book I would suddenly be holding it in my hands and be able to read it in the pleasant shade, and so on and so forth.

Everything could appear here except for two things: snakes and chicken brains. When I managed to explain to the purple people what that was, they laughed. Yes, they could actually laugh, and they often did.

Then one day there was an indescribably lovely creature in front of me, looking at me through its dark purple eyes. By instinct I reached my hand out toward her – I perceived it as being *a she*, but it could have been a he if I had perceived it that way – and she did likewise.

When our hands touched, her face lit up with the kind of joy that could only be compared to the joy I saw in my own face when I looked toward The Mirror which, from the planet's side, only reflected the things that are on that planet.

Even though it could also do otherwise if someone wanted. But no one did.

I have stayed on here, purple person that I am.

My Dying Wish I Will Grant Myself

Professor Emeritus Roman Block died old and no one was particularly sad about it. Yet his passing did attract attention. For two reasons, you might say. The first reason was that he was not found lifeless in his apartment until three weeks after he had died. In the beginning, people who knew his children and grandchildren were very judgmental. How could they go so long without visiting their father and grandfather when they lived only a few hundred yards from his home?

"For God's sake, he's been rotting away in the apartment for a month!" some said.

"Shameless!" said others.

Roman's children defended themselves by claiming something nobody wanted to believe. At least not before the letter left by Professor Block had been published. That was the second reason people paid attention to his death.

The letter read as follows:

"It is not death that I fear, but the way I'll be treated afterwards.

When a star falls, it is said that a person has died. After all, the star burns up and turns to ash. It comes to an end. It has no ability to reflect on that fact before it dies. What about a human being? What choice does a human have? Well, he has two choices: to be buried or cremated. What happens if he doesn't want either one? Nothing, those are the only two options on offer.

I have shuddered at both of these options nearly my whole life. What if I am only clinically dead and wake up after I am buried? What happens if I wake up just as the crematory is fired up? Which may seem laughable to those reading this. Not to me! Nor are these mere rhetorical questions for me. Such thoughts give me anxiety, and I have considered these matters more than once.

The idea behind my dying wish emerged from these misgivings. But I knew that no one would accept my dying wish regarding the handling of my remains after my death. And I could understand that. I myself would have a hard time accepting it if it were someone else's wish. So I had no choice but to grant my own wish.

When I was diagnosed with cancer and told that I only had three months to live, I decided on the only possible course, the only way that would set me at ease.

One month before I was going to die (I had a strong feeling about this), I told my children and grandchildren that I was going to fly to Majorca and stay there for four weeks. They had no inkling of my approaching death and were a bit surprised at my sudden trip, since I was not someone known for being keen on travel. But they couldn't do anything about it. In their eyes I looked fit and healthy, and it wasn't their money I was going to spend for that matter. I lied to them and said I had already bought the ticket and that they did not need to accompany me to the airport. They insisted. I insisted even more and they gave up. What were they going to do? Who was going to persuade a stubborn old man like me?

My idea was to die alone and to not be discovered before my remains had decomposed to the point that my death could not be doubted. My first thought was to venture into a forest and do it there. I then decided against it for various reasons. I hid in my apartment and awaited death. I had enough food. I didn't need much, since I was dying and was able to eat only a fraction of what I had when healthy. I needed morphine more than food, and I had it.

When my loved ones called me up I lied, first by telling them that I had arrived, then that my days on Majorca were happy and eventful, and finally that I would be back in two days and that one of them was welcome to come by my place to see what a deep tan I had managed to achieve.

Sure, I had qualms about what I had done to them and the shock they were in for, but my fear of being buried alive or incinerated was several times stronger than my pangs of conscience. I simply could not subject myself to all the dark and agonizing scenarios I would concoct before I died: scenes of coming to in the grave and not being able to breathe or move, of waking up in the crematory and waiting to be burned alive. No, I didn't want to think about that. I don't want to bring that kind of misfortune on myself.

PS

I'm dying now. In peace and quiet. All shot up with morphine. With lots of fragrant flowers underneath, around and on top of my dying, and soon to be decaying, body.

Dying with the memory of all the happy days I have experienced in my long life.

Here I lie free on the floor of my apartment, abandoning it to the natural, risk-free and final process of dissolution.

Like an animal in the forest. Like a deer or a squirrel or hedgehog. Doesn't matter what animal.

Nothing matters now. I die without any cares whatsoever.

I have nothing more to say... "

About the Author

Predrag Mihajlović was born in the former Yugoslavia. He has lived in Sweden since 1992. He is a lawyer, literary scholar and teacher. He currently teaches Swedish as a second language. He made his debut with the short story *Apatriden och den förvirrade hunden* in 2017. The short story is also available in English translation (*The Apatride and the Confused Dog*) and in Serbian translation (*Apatrid i zbunjeni pas)*. The same year also saw the publication of his short novel *Skuggor och eldflugor*, which is also available in Serbian translation (*Sjene i svici*). This collection of short stories, **Stella Canis and Other Short Stories** (*Stella Canis och andra noveller),* is his third book.